D0116293

Greenley: A Tree's Story

Joanne Randolph

alphabet soup™
an imprint of

WINDMILL
BOOKS™
New York

For Riley, Deming, and Hannah—my own little saplings, and the apples of my eye

Published in 2009 by Windmill Books, LLC
303 Park Avenue South, Suite # 1280, New York, NY 10010-3657

First Edition

Book Design and Illustrations by: Planman Technologies (India) Pvt. Ltd.

Publisher Cataloging Data

Randolph, Joanne
      Greenley : a tree's story / by Joanne Randolph.
p.   cm. – (Nature stories)
Summary: Greenley the apple tree tells how he grew from a seed inside an apple
his mother dropped on the ground into a big tree making apples of his own.
ISBN 978-1-60754-089-2 (lib.) – ISBN 978-1-60754-090-8 (pbk.)
ISBN 978-1-60754-091-5 (6-pack)
      1. Apple tree—Juvenile fiction [1. Apple tree—Fiction 2. Trees—Fiction
3. Seeds—Fiction
 I. Title II. Series
      [E]—dc22

Manufactured in the United States of America

Hey, there! My name is Greenley! I am an apple tree! Would you like to know what it's like to be an apple tree? I can tell you all about myself and my family tree.

I bet you've tasted an apple before, haven't you? Well, growing apples is what I do best! I learned it from my mom. She is tall with leafy green hair. In the fall she has the most beautiful, red jewelry ever—apples!

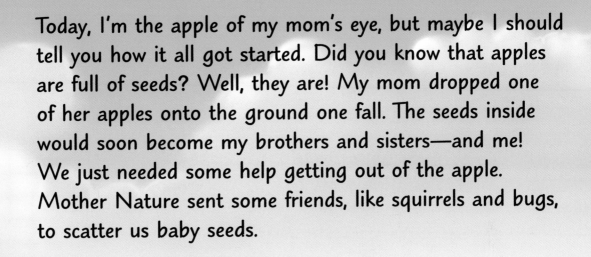

Today, I'm the apple of my mom's eye, but maybe I should tell you how it all got started. Did you know that apples are full of seeds? Well, they are! My mom dropped one of her apples onto the ground one fall. The seeds inside would soon become my brothers and sisters—and me! We just needed some help getting out of the apple. Mother Nature sent some friends, like squirrels and bugs, to scatter us baby seeds.

Once I was out of the apple, I planted myself in the ground and waited. It was a long, cold winter underground, but the weather finally started to warm up. It was springtime!

My mom told me to reach for the Sun. So I started to stretch. I sent a little sprout up from the ground and pretty soon, I grew into a nice little sapling. Mom told me to make sure to spread my roots into the ground. I know you and your friends like to run around, but trees like to stay in one place. My roots are like my feet, and, boy, are my feet important!

11

Are your mom and dad always telling you to eat your vegetables? Well, I need water and minerals to help me grow big and strong, too. I don't eat and drink with my mouth like you do, though. I use my *feet, or roots,* to pull vitamins and water from the ground. That's why they're so important. Plus I'd fall over without them!

My roots send all the water and minerals up my trunk and to my leaves. But if you think my roots are amazing, just wait until you hear about my leaves! I can use water, sunlight, and air, plus the green coloring in my leaves to make my own food! No trips to the grocery store for me.

I spend all spring working on growing bigger and getting ready to make apples. My mom and I like to dress our best in spring. We cover ourselves in flowers and new leaves. We make lots of new friends, like bees and butterflies. They help us make our apples by bringing a special dust called pollen with them. I bet your friends help you out sometimes, too.

In the summer, all of our leaves have grown in. The petals fall off my flowers, but the inner part of the flower holds onto my branches and starts to grow bigger. Then just wait and see what happens!

19

Fall is showtime! At last, our flowers turn into beautiful apples that are grown and ready for picking.

When it starts getting cold out, it's time for me to drop my leaves and the rest of my apples and get ready for my winter's sleep.

Spring

Summer

Winter

Fall

I'll wake up again in the spring to get ready to make some more apples. I hope I'll see you then. But, whenever you see an apple tree, remember to say hello and tell them you're a friend of Greenley's!

For more great fiction and nonfiction,
go to windmillbooks.com.